DISNEY
PRINCESS
BEGINNINGS

CINDERELLA
Takes the Stage

BY TESSA ROEHL

ILLUSTRATED BY
THE DISNEY STORYBOOK ART TEAM

For anyone who believes in magic.
—T. R.

Copyright © 2017 Disney Enterprises, Inc. All rights reserved. Published in the United States by Random House Children's Books, a division of Penguin Random House LLC, 1745 Broadway, New York, NY 10019, and in Canada by Penguin Random House Canada Limited, Toronto, in conjunction with Disney Enterprises, Inc. Random House and the colophon are registered trademarks of Penguin Random House LLC.

randomhousekids.com

Library of Congress Cataloging-in-Publication Data is available upon request.

ISBN 978-0-7364-3578-9 (trade) — ISBN 978-0-7364-8176-2 (lib. bdg.)

Printed in the United States of America

10 9 8 7 6 5 4 3 2 1

This book has been officially leveled by using the F&P Text Level Gradient™ Leveling System.

Chapter 1
A Fairy in the Willow

Ella stared into the willow tree, looking for a twinkle, a glow, or the movement of wings. "Are you sure there are fairies in this tree, Mother?" Ella asked.

"Yes, quite sure," her mother replied.

Ella frowned. The only wings she could see belonged to the songbirds. Ella came to this bench every day to watch the animals. She was sure if there were fairies around, she would have noticed. But just in case, she looked harder.

This was Ella's favorite corner of the garden because there was a feeling here that anything was possible. In this corner, a pear tree had borne fruit after a winter's frost, a rabbit had nibbled a berry right from her hand, and two hazel branches had grown twisting around each other, as if they couldn't stand to be apart.

That Ella could also see the highest tower of the king's castle from her garden bench didn't hurt either. With a view of a place where royalty lived, ruling so lovingly over Ella's tiny kingdom, it was easy to get swept

away in daydreams. The songbirds knew all

about Ella's dreams, because sometimes she

simply had to tell someone.

She would tell the birds about the castle's

magnificent sparkling staircase. She'd heard

that it was just inside the Grand Hall. Someday, she said, she would float down the steps while someone very important announced her name.

She would tell the birds about the dress, too. It would be made of silver and gold fabric, just like the one in the window of the village dressmaker's shop. The one she would buy with the money she planned to win at the Midsummer Festival Puppet Contest.

The birds would only chirp in reply. And they never told Ella any of their dreams. So she often wished for a different kind of friend to share her dreams with.

On days like this, when Ella found herself

wishing for things that were not there, she was glad to have the company of her mother—even if she was just talking about fairies she couldn't see.

One thing Ella could see was an army of ants marching across the garden, right in the path of her shoe. The thought of all those tiny feet crawling up her stocking made Ella squirm.

Ella gathered her legs to her chest as the ants scurried into their anthill. But before she could return her shoes to the ground, she noticed that one ant was left behind, running in circles around the base of the bench.

"Ella, dear," her mother said. "Has this little ant frightened you?"

"I don't want it to crawl on me," Ella said, still hugging her knees.

Ella's mother pointed to the ant. "Who might be the more terrified one in this garden? The one who has lost sight of his family and forgotten his way? Or you, with your size and your mother to protect you?"

She opened her fan, which she always carried on warm days like this one. Blue and red painted petunias blossomed against thin cream paper.

She laid the fan against the ground. The ant crawled into a fold, and Ella's mother carried it to the anthill.

The ant disappeared into the dirt.

"Everyone deserves a happy ending," her mother said as she sat back down.

"I don't mind the ants. I just don't want to touch them," Ella said.

Ella's mother pulled her close. "Ella, when you were new to the world, I would bring you out to this bench and sing to you every morning."

"I like it when you sing." Ella rested her head on her mother's shoulder. She hoped the ant had found its way back to its own mother.

"I sang so that the fairies would listen. I sang songs about my dreams for you, hoping there might be a fairy who would take a special interest in my little Ella. And then, one day, a fairy did."

"In me?" Ella's eyes opened wide.

"She flew out of the willow tree, dressed in a blue frock. She asked if she could be your fairy godmother," Ella's mother said.

Ella had never heard of such a thing. "And what did you say?"

"Silly dear. I said yes!" Ella's mother laughed. "And she said, 'Tell Ella, this is her fairy godmother's tree. Should she ever need some magic, she'll know where to find it.'"

"Is this a real story?" Ella looked up at her mother's smiling face.

"Do you want it to be real, my darling?" her mother asked.

"Of course I do!" Ella exclaimed.

"So then it's real. Anything can be real if you believe it." Ella's mother winked.

Ella considered this. "But, Mother. Why did you want the fairies to take an interest in me?"

"I will always be looking out for you,

my Ella," her mother said. "But I knew it wouldn't hurt if someone with a touch of magic was looking out for you as well. We must always look out for others. Especially the smallest creatures."

"Arf!" A bark followed by a series of loud, splashing crashes sounded across the garden.

"And speaking of small creatures." Ella's mother stood. "I think your new puppy could use some looking after."

Ella sighed as her mother left the garden. Bruno had knocked over several watering cans, creating a perfect, puppy-sized mud pit. And Bruno liked mud.

"Oh, Bruno." Ella picked him up, careful

to avoid his dirty fur.
She couldn't help
smiling as she carried
him to the barn. He whined but stayed still
as she washed him.

"Now, let's hurry up and have lunch," Ella
told him. "No more playing about with fairies
for me, and no more playing about with mud
for you. I have to finish my puppets in time
to win the contest." Bruno barked in response
and then bounded up the path behind her,
toward the chateau.

Chapter 2
An Unwanted Visitor

Ella entered the dining room just as her parents were sitting down at the table. She eyed the platter in the middle: roasted fish and vegetables—it wasn't her favorite meal, but it was certainly one of Bruno's.

Ella kissed her father on the cheek as she headed toward the kitchen to retrieve Bruno's lunch. She hadn't taken two steps before Florence, the cook, appeared with Bruno's bowl in her hands.

"Thank you, Florence. Bruno thanks you, too!" Ella took the bowl and placed it under the table. Florence smiled at Ella and retreated to the kitchen. Ella looked at the colorless mush that made up Bruno's lunch. She'd make sure to sneak him some of the fish.

Ella took her place at the table next to her mother.

She loaded her plate with a small portion and chewed fast enough that she wouldn't taste it. In no time, her plate was empty.

"All that chatting in the garden with your mother worked up an appetite, did it, Ella?" Her father looked at her, amused. He wasn't even halfway done with his serving.

"There's really no time to waste, Father. If I'm going to win the puppet contest, every minute counts," Ella said. She scooped a bit more of the fish onto her plate. As her father leaned in for another bite, Ella sneaked a piece down to Bruno's waiting mouth.

"It's hard to believe you're already old enough to enter," Ella's mother said.

"I've only been waiting for this my entire life!" Ella said. "It's my favorite time of year."

Ella's mother chuckled. "We know it's your favorite, darling. When you were younger, I had a terrible time pulling you away from the festival bonfires. You were so enchanted that you would come home covered in cinders."

"Cinders?" Ella asked. "I love the bonfires, but I don't remember getting dirty."

"I remember," Ella's father chimed in.

"Your father had to rinse you off, just like you were a puppy splashing in the mud." Ella's mother tousled Ella's hair. "Our little Cinderella."

Ella scowled playfully. Bruno licked her hand below the table, tasting fish. Ella was hoping she would be excused—soon.

"How are your puppets coming along?" Ella's father asked.

"They're all right. I'm having a touch of trouble making them look the way they do in my head." Ella was stretching the truth. She was actually having nothing but trouble.

"I do wish I could help you," her mother said. "I never took to sewing myself. It just wasn't my cup of tea, I suppose."

"I'll sort it out. How hard can it be to make little costumes and little puppets?"

Ella asked. She slipped one more bite of fish to Bruno and then fidgeted in her chair.

"You're excused, Ella. Run along to work your magic," Ella's father said, as if reading her mind. "I brought a couple of things for you from the village, by the way. They're on the desk in my study."

Ella leaped up from her chair. "Oh, thank you, Father!" She hurried to the desk. Folded on top were a piece of plum-colored velvet and a length of black ribbon. They would be perfect for the frog puppet's suit.

With her new materials in hand, Ella left the house and ran toward the barn. Bruno trailed behind.

"Good luck, my Cinderella!" Ella heard her mother call from an open window. Ella turned back and waved.

The chickens clucked around Ella's ankles as she passed.

"I know you've all had your lunch already." Ella winked at the birds and dipped her hand into a pail of corn. She tossed a handful onto the ground. Bruno tried to pick up some kernels, but the chickens kept beating him to it. Ella wagged her finger at him. "If you get extra lunch today, I think they should, too."

Inside the barn, Ella made her way to the corner where she'd set up her workplace. She added the new fabric and ribbon to the pile of other materials:

ribbons and beads,

pieces of linen,

MORE trimmings,

and a handful of buttons.

It was everything Ella needed to make beautiful puppets.

If only she could actually make them.

Ella tried not to look at the other pile on the table. It was a collection of misshapen puppet heads and tiny costumes filled with holes from her frustrated stitches. She sat down on her stool, set her shoulders back, and held her head high. No matter about the pile of mistakes. Ella was certain she could figure out how to fix them.

She picked up the puppet that was supposed to be the maiden. It looked more like a potato.

She had just set to ripping out the stitches when she heard a clatter outside the barn. Ella dropped the puppet. She turned around to scold Bruno for whatever he had gotten into this time, but Bruno was right there on the ground, snoozing.

Ella ran to the barn door and saw what had caused the commotion. Next to the doorway was a metal bucket of discarded scraps. The bucket was lying on its side — and it was empty. Ella looked around to see what animal might have knocked it over. But instead she saw a girl running away toward the trees beyond the chateau gate.

Thief! Ella thought. And before she had time to think anything else, Ella sprinted after her.

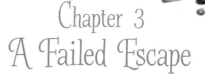

Chapter 3
A Failed Escape

"Hey! Come back!" Ella shouted as she ran. The excitement had awakened Bruno, and he raced alongside her. The girl disappeared into the trees just as Ella reached the edge of the woods. Ella wasn't used to chasing people, or going into the woods, for that matter. She was about to turn back when she saw the girl again. The thief had stopped running. She was standing, hands on hips, only a few trees away.

Ella marched toward the thief. As she got closer, she could see that the girl's clothes were tattered, her face was grubby, and her short, dark hair was chopped unevenly. She didn't seem to notice as Ella approached.

The girl was just looking at the ground and . . . talking to it?

"Excuse me! What do you think you're— Oh!" Ella had reached the thief, who wasn't talking to the ground at all. She was talking to a small, brown-spotted pig whose foot was caught on a tree root. Bruno sniffed the pig.

"Now look what you've done, Claudio," the thief said to the pig. The pig squealed in response.

"Surely it's not his fault," Ella said, forgetting for a moment why she had chased the girl into the forest. "Here, if both of us pull on the root, I think we can give him enough space to wiggle out."

The two girls grabbed hold of the root and tugged as hard as they could. It was thick and tough, but it rose enough to give Claudio room to move. He didn't budge, however. He stayed there, staring at Ella.

"Claudio, enough! Move!" the thief urged her pig. Bruno let out one of his best barks.

Claudio squealed and jumped away from the root.

"That's a good boy," Ella said to the pig, holding her hand out to say hello.

Claudio nuzzled her palm and let out a soft snort.

"This is all his fault." The thief gave Claudio a scratch under his chin. "He does this kind of thing on purpose. Doesn't think it's right to run away and all that. This pig's morals are too strong for his own good," the thief said as she picked Claudio up and plopped him in her bag.

Ella suddenly remembered she was angry. "Well, at least one of you has some morals. What gives you the right to steal from me?"

The thief rolled her eyes. "Steal? That wasn't stealing. You weren't using those scraps. You were throwing them away!"

"That doesn't make them yours!" Ella said.

"It doesn't matter anyway. You can have them back." The thief dug into the satchel slung over her shoulder. It was actually a flour sack attached to an old leather belt. "I didn't even realize what I was taking. I could have saved us both some trouble, because these are definitely not my taste—Cinderella."

She shoved a handful of the discarded beads and fabric toward Ella, who accepted them with a huff.

The thief stomped off in the direction of the village. Bruno barked after them. "Hush, Bruno. They're not your friends," Ella scolded him. From over the thief's shoulder, Claudio snorted at Ella and Bruno. He really was quite cute. Ella shook her head. Never mind. She stomped back home.

Chapter 4
A Search in the Village

Ella arrived back at the chateau to find her parents having tea in the sitting room. She was out of breath from her chase into the woods and her angry return. She flung herself onto the sofa.

"Well, that was a short work session," Ella's father said as he stirred a spoonful of sugar into his teacup.

"I didn't do any work," Ella grumbled.

Ella's mother crossed the room and put her hand to Ella's cheek. "Darling, are you all right? Your face is flushed."

Ella patted her mother's hand. "That's because I've been chasing down a thief when I ought to have been perfecting my puppets."

Seeing her parents' confused faces, Ella told them the story of her encounter with the girl in the woods: from the clattering bucket, to the stuck pig, to her retreat. "I'm too distracted now to get any work done today," she finished. "And it's all her fault."

Ella's parents exchanged a look. The kind of look they didn't think Ella noticed, but she always did. It meant they knew something Ella didn't.

"What?" Ella asked. "Why aren't you as angry as I am? Don't you think stealing is wrong?"

Ella's father cleared his throat and set down his tea. "Ella, my sunshine, it's true that these were materials you discarded."

"But that doesn't give her the right—" Ella began.

Her father held up a hand, silencing her. "Ella, you'll often find that people deserve more than one encounter before you rush to judgment. This girl, whom you call a thief, why, she's more than just a thief. She's a pig owner. She's a forest traveler. You can't know that she meant you harm when she took your scraps." Ella's father handed her a cup of tea. "There's good in everyone. You just have to know where to find it," he added.

Ella tasted her tea. Her father always made it just right, with the perfect amount of milk and sugar.

"What do you think, dear? Do you hear what your father is saying?" Ella's mother asked.

"Yes, Mother. Yes, Father. I hear you." Ella continued sipping her tea. *Good in everyone?* she thought. The look on the thief's face when she sneered at Ella's scraps—that wasn't very good.

Yes, Ella heard her parents. But she didn't have to agree.

The next morning when Ella woke, her father's words were still on her mind. They had been there all night, worming their way into her dreams. She also couldn't stop picturing the face of the little pig, Claudio. He really was cute. And so small. Considering the thief's shabby appearance,

Ella worried whether the pig had enough to eat.

She decided that instead of her morning daydream in the garden, she'd go to the village to find poor, possibly hungry Claudio. Ella slurped down her breakfast, rushed to help her mother with the chores, and gathered a small bag of grain. She had just set off down the path to the village when Bruno trotted up beside her.

"Bruno," Ella said as she stopped. "Wouldn't you rather stay home and play in the garden? I won't be gone long."

Bruno licked Ella's hands and wagged his tail.

Ella thought for a moment. "You've never been to the village before. You'll have to stay out of trouble. But maybe you can help sniff out that pig and make sure he knows we're his friends. Do you think you can do that?"

Bruno yelped and wagged his tail harder.

"All right, then. Come along, and keep your eyes and nose out for Claudio."

Ella and Bruno continued down the path. Bruno paused every few steps to enjoy a new scent. "I think you'll like the village," Ella said as they walked. "There are many things to smell, people to meet, and crumbs to eat. Just don't get any ideas about making a mess."

They reached the first line of shops, and Ella tried not to feel nervous. She rarely went to the village alone, and she wasn't sure where to begin. All she had was a description of a girl and a pig.

Gathering her courage, she approached the first person she saw: a man selling fresh bread from his cart.

"Excuse me, have you seen a girl with short, dark hair? Kind of dirty, wears a flour sack, and carries a pet pig?" As she spoke, Ella realized there couldn't possibly be more than one person who fit that description.

"Hmmm." The man thought. "Girl, yes. Pig, no. Try the west side of the village. I believe she comes from that direction."

Ella gave a little curtsy. "Thank you."

She and Bruno headed west. As they went, she asked a few more people. Again, no one had seen Claudio, but they seemed familiar with the girl. One shopkeeper pointed Ella toward a large estate looming atop a small hill.

Ella was sure he was mistaken. She couldn't imagine the thief living in such a grand home. But with nothing else to go on, Ella and Bruno headed up the drive. As they approached the gate, Ella began quietly calling out, "Claudio! Claudio!"

They were almost to the top of the hill. Bruno's ears pricked up and his nose twitched. It seemed they were getting closer. "Claudio!" Ella cried a bit louder.

Suddenly, the thief appeared in front of her. And before Ella knew it, she was being yanked off the drive.

Chapter 5
Metal, Moss, and Stone

Ella had been pulled into a small room. Or not just a room. A one-room home. A shack, really. The thief stood in front of Ella, her face angry. Bruno nosed open the door and sauntered inside, heading for a bed against the wall.

"What do you think you're doing?" Ella asked the thief.

"What am *I* doing? What do you think

you're doing?" the thief responded, hands on hips.

"I was looking for Claudio," Ella said. As she spoke his name, the little pig crawled out from under the bed. There was only one in the room, as well as a small stove, a modest table with two chairs, and curtains draped across a corner.

That was it. *Does someone really live here?* Ella wondered.

"Listen, you can't go around shouting his name." The thief picked up the pig, and he snuffled her cheek. She placed a hand over Claudio's head, covering his ears. "My mother and I live here. We take care of all the animals on the property: pigs, sheep, cows, chickens. The master of the estate can't know about Claudio."

"Why not? Did you steal him, too?" Ella asked, putting her hands on her hips.

"Stealing isn't always bad, you know." The thief pressed her hands harder against the pig's ears. "Claudio was born to a pair of the estate owner's prized pigs. He was the tiniest runt any of us had ever seen. The instant Sir Edgard saw him, he ordered my mother to"—the girl shuddered—"dispose of him. Of course we couldn't do that. So I took him. Sir Edgard can't find out, or I don't know what he'll do."

Ella could not believe what she was hearing. Not just the story about Claudio, but the name: Sir Edgard. Ella was sure she'd heard it before. Then it dawned on her. "Why, Sir Edgard! The judge of the puppet contest? That Sir Edgard?"

The girl narrowed her eyes at Ella. "The very one. I'm not even so sure he's a sir.

He certainly tells us to call him that, but I can't imagine the good king making that awful man a sir."

"Oh, my." Ella couldn't stand to think that the man who had been cruel to Claudio would be the same person to judge her puppets. But what could she do about it? She handed the bag of grain to the girl. "Anyway. This is why I came. I wanted to make sure Claudio had enough to eat."

The girl looked at the gift. Claudio struggled in her arms to peek into the bag. "He does just fine. Claudio eats even before my mother and I do. But thank you anyway."

Ella shrugged and headed for the door. The girl called after her. "Wait. I'm sorry. I didn't introduce myself. My name is Val, short for Valentine."

Ella turned. "You know, my name isn't actually Cinderella. That was just a silly name you must have heard my mother call me. My real name is Ella."

Val waved her hand as if to dismiss what Ella said. "You really ought to stick with Cinderella, for the contest. You're entering, right? I never go by Valentine, but that's what I'm using for the contest. It's a much better puppeteer name, and so is Cinderella. Mademoiselle Cinderella."

Ella was surprised. "You're entering the contest?"

Val set Claudio on the floor, along with the bag of grain. Bruno had been waiting at her feet for the pig and sniffed him hello. "Can I show you something?"

"Of course." Ella was curious.

Val walked to the curtains hanging in the corner and pulled them to the side. A stack of crates was shoved against the wall, piled high with various puppets. Puppets like Ella had never seen before. Made from materials she had never seen before. Where Ella had been using fabric, thread, stuffing,

and lace, Val's puppets were made from all kinds of materials.

"Your puppets—they're glorious," Ella could only whisper.

"They're getting there," Val said. "Thank you, though. Once I win the contest, I plan to buy a goat with the gold coin."

"A goat?" Ella crinkled her nose. She thought it seemed like a strange prize.

Val nodded, excited. "My mother has been saving to buy a farm out in the country. So we can get away from Sir Edgard once and for all. Of course, that's a long way off, considering how little he pays her. He's always finding reasons to dock her wages, too. A goat would be a good start. One animal of our own. Besides Claudio."

Ella had never thought about what it might be like to want to escape your home and start again somewhere new. But it made sense for Val. "Well, if you can finish them, you might have a good chance at winning."

Val sighed. "Yes. I wish I had more room to work. But I'll get them done. I believe it."

Ella wanted to touch the puppets and examine them. She wanted to see how Val managed to sew leaves together when Ella couldn't even attach a button. Then an idea formed in Ella's mind. "Val, I have a proposal for you."

"You have a proposal for a thief?" Val smirked.

"I think there's a way we can help each other," Ella said.

"I'm listening, Cinderella."

Ella smiled. "I'm having a little . . . trouble working with my materials. Sewing anything, really. If you show me some of your tricks, I'd like to offer you space in my barn to work on your puppets. There's plenty of room for both of us! And I promise I won't copy your ideas, as long as you don't copy mine."

Val chuckled. "I've got plenty of ideas. I won't be taking yours." She scratched her head, thinking. "It's a deal!" she said, sticking out her hand.

Ella shook Val's hand, pleased with her own clever thinking. "Excellent. I'll see you tomorrow morning, first thing."

"Claudio and I will be there!" Val said. Claudio didn't look up from the food he was devouring.

Ella and Bruno left the shack. Val's puppets were going to be hard to beat. But Ella still believed her own puppets could win. Now that she would have help, she was sure she was closer than ever to winning the gold coin. As they walked back through the village toward the chateau, she waved at the dress in the window that would soon be hers.

Chapter 6
An Unusual Set of Tools

The next morning, just after breakfast, Val arrived at the chateau, pulling a makeshift wagon. It was filled to the brim with puppet parts and other odds and ends. Ella couldn't wait to see how Val would use the strange assortment of things.

"Where do you want us?" Val asked, lifting Claudio out of the flour satchel on her shoulder. The pig ran into the barn as if he'd lived there for years. Bruno followed him, sniffing eagerly all the way.

"Here." Ella took the wagon handle from Val and walked inside, where she'd set up a table identical to her own.

"Wow. There sure is a lot of space." Val unloaded her cart, piling up pieces of wood, broken door handles, chain links, part of a horse blanket, flower petals, and more. Ella tried not to stare, but she was curious.

"Oh!" Val jumped back, dropping the broken leather shoe she was unpacking. "Hello?"

A furry brown head had popped up in the pile of Val's supplies.

"That's just one of the barn mice," Ella said. "They're quite friendly!"

The mouse scurried into the pile. "No problem, mouse," Val said. "You may want to avoid this table. It could be dangerous if you dart over here while I'm hammering."

"Hammering?" Ella shook her head in amazement. She sat down at her own table and picked up the maiden puppet, which still looked like a potato. She squished the stuffed shape near the bottom. She hoped if she attacked it with a needle and thread, she might be able to form a neck. A neck that would lead to a head.

After she'd jabbed the puppet a few

times, she noticed that the clanking and scraping of Val's unloading had stopped. Ella turned and startled. Val was right behind her, watching her hands.

"I see your problem, Cinderella," Val said, a smile forming on her face.

"Am I completely hopeless?" Ella asked.

Val shook her head and sat down. "You just need some basics."

Val showed Ella how to begin a stitch and how to knot it at the end. In no time, Val had a neat, strong seam forming a neck that looked like a neck. Then a head that looked like a head. Ella paid close attention.

"How would you sew something like

this?" Ella held up a piece of her favorite fabric, a shiny lavender silk. Part of it was covered in holes where Ella had accidentally torn the fabric with her needle.

"Well, that's very delicate." Val retrieved some things from her supplies and brought them to Ella. "Take this rose petal, for example. Not an easy thing to sew with that large metal needle. But this can keep it from tearing." Val pulled a thin threaded pine needle through the rose petal, creating a few perfect stitches down the middle. "Try it!"

"A pine needle!" Ella was shocked. Val was full of surprises.

"Of course!" Val said. "You'd be surprised

what makes itself available to you when you're in need. I use all the tools at my disposal. Even if they don't seem like tools at first." Val smiled. She gave Ella a handful of pine needles and sat back down to her own puppets.

"Now, where is the thread I wanted to use for this silk? It's a lovely blue. It looks like a wisp of sky." Ella searched through her things. Another barn mouse crept out from under some fabric. The spool of sky-blue thread was balanced on his head. "Why, thank you," Ella told the mouse as she took the spool.

Ella picked up one of the pine needles. She wasn't sure how Val had made such a perfect hole for the thread. The mouse sat, watching Ella think. His eyes were bright and curious. "Any ideas?" Ella asked the mouse as she held the needle out for him to see. The mouse bit into the end of the pine needle and scurried away before Ella could react.

She looked at the needle. The mouse's tooth had made a tiny hole in the end—just the right size. Ella threaded the pine needle and poked it through the silk. She found that even when she tugged, the fabric stayed in one piece. "It's working. You're a genius, Val!"

"I can't disagree with you," Val said.

"Where did you learn all this?" Ella asked

as she continued weaving the pine needle through the fabric. She was making what she hoped would be the maiden's skirt.

"My mother taught me ages ago. If she didn't, I wouldn't have any clothes to wear!" Val spoke between loud bangs as she beat a brick with a hammer.

Ella couldn't imagine what she was going to do with pieces of brick.

"Sorry," Val said. "Is this noise going to bother you?"

Ella shook her head. "If you want, I really do have plenty of materials here. You're welcome to use some of them."

"No thanks." Val returned to her brick.

"They're very pretty. But I think I have a style of my own going here. Now that I have room to actually swing my hammer."

Ella finished the hem of the skirt. The next step in her plan was a lace top. She began looking for a piece of lace, but stopped. *Use all the tools at your disposal.* "Excuse me, little mouse? Are you there?"

The mouse curiously crawled out of the fabric pile.

"Do you happen to know where the ivory lace is? I think I brought it in a couple of days ago," Ella told the mouse, who darted back into the pile. He returned moments later, the lace in his teeth. Ella was delighted. "Why, thank you! Do you have a name?"

The mouse stared at her, whiskers twitching.

"I see. Well, let's call you Leopold. Leo for short," Ella said as she patted his head.

The mouse bowed and ran back to the mound of materials, squeaking. Ella could have sworn that the squeak sounded just like the mouse had said, "Good day, Cinderella."

Ella turned to Val.
"Did you hear that?
I'm sure that mouse
spoke to me. Have you ever heard a mouse
speak?"

"Hmm, I don't think so." Val shrugged.
"Maybe a fairy charmed him."

The girls continued working for hours,
pausing only for the soup Florence brought
them for lunch. Val sewed and hammered
and fastened. Ella sewed and cut and beaded.

By the time the sun was low in the sky,
Ella's maiden puppet was nearly finished.
The girls took a break for tea and biscuits
brought out by Ella's father. He didn't say a

word to interrupt. He just gave the two girls, Claudio, and Bruno pats on the head and a tip of his hat.

"So, what would you do with the prize money, Mademoiselle Cinderella?" Val asked as she sipped her tea.

"What *will* I do with the prize money, you mean?" Ella grinned.

"I admit you've made a lot of progress. But I have a trick up my sleeve that will guarantee me the win," Val said.

"Oh, do you?" Ella took a sip of tea. "It's not just about the gold coin for me. The Midsummer Festival is my favorite day of the year. There's so much magic in the air. And the puppets are the best part—besides the bonfires, of course." She paused. For some reason, she felt silly telling Val about the dress. "But the prize is a bonus. I've had my eye on a dress in the village. I guess that might seem less important than a goat."

Val's eyes lit up. "Is it the gold-and-silver one? In the window of Madame Colette's?"

"Yes!" Ella was surprised. Val didn't seem like the type to care about a dress. She could make such beautiful things herself.

"It's absolutely gorgeous. It would look stunning with your hair," Val said.

Ella blushed.

Val continued. "I don't think a dream of winning a dress is any less important than a dream of winning a goat. We should all get the chance, right? Our hearts don't always need to want the same thing. As long as they want something."

Ella felt much better. Val understood. "Exactly," Ella said.

"I'm just sorry your dream won't come true this year," Val said with a smirk Ella now knew well.

"Oh, you." Ella threw a handful of hay at Val.

"Thank you! This will make fabulous puppet hair," Val said, giggling.

The girls finished their tea. Claudio and Bruno were fast asleep on the hay after a day of playing. Val scooped the sleeping Claudio into her bag, and held out her hand for Ella to shake. "Same time tomorrow?" Val asked.

"Same time," Ella said. She waved good-bye as Val and Claudio trotted down the path toward the village. Ella felt warm inside, and it wasn't only from the tea.

Chapter 7
A Partner in Puppets and Dreams

The next day, Val showed up again, as promised. And the day after that, and the day after that—and every day leading up to the festival.

Val and Ella worked side by side. They talked about everything. Val told Ella about living with her mother on Sir Edgard's estate. Val's mother used to care for the animals with Val's father, and each earned a salary. After Val's father died, Val's mother had to take on double the work—but Sir Edgard refused to give her double the pay. Val tried to help her mother whenever she could, but Sir Edgard felt he was so important that he wouldn't speak to Val directly. He would pass orders to her through her mother, saying things like "Tell the child this" or "Tell the child that."

Val told Ella about what her future farm would look like: not too big and not too small. There would be some geese, a cow, some chickens, and Val's goat, to start. Val talked about how peaceful the farm would be. She and her mother would feel so free. There would be no one like Sir Edgard to give them orders. The work they did would be only for themselves.

In turn, Ella shared her dreams with Val. She told Val of her morning visits to the garden, looking for the fairies and gazing at the castle. How she pictured herself dancing in the castle ballroom or even atop one of the clouds in the sky. Ella also dreamed of experiencing a great adventure someday. The kind of adventure that might be written down in books like the ones she read with her father in his study. She told Val how she couldn't wait to grow up and see more of the world beyond their lovely but small kingdom.

It occurred to Ella that only days before, she had been sitting in the garden, longing for someone to talk to and share her dreams with. And maybe she had stumbled upon a pocket of magic, because that very person had entered her life. As Val had said, *You'd be surprised what makes itself available to you when you're in need.* Ella hadn't even realized how much she needed Val, but here Val was all the same.

Bruno and Claudio also had become fast friends. They would dart around the beams and buckets and piles of hay, playing hide-and-seek and sharing bits of food. Then they would curl up together to nap in the warm afternoon sun that shone through the barn window.

That was how it went day after day. As Claudio and Bruno played and napped, Ella and Val chatted and worked. All the while, Val would offer Ella tips on how to craft her puppets. Leo and the rest of the barn mice proved helpful as well. They would line up with the exact materials Ella needed before she even knew to look for them. Soon Ella had nearly all her puppets complete.

There were a frog, a maiden,

a fairy, and a tree.

Ella couldn't figure out what Val's puppets were supposed to be, and Val wouldn't tell her. All Ella knew was that it didn't matter. They were magnificent. Ella kept offering Val some of her beads or trimmings or fabric. Val kept refusing, always saying something like "I've got everything I need. Don't worry about me, Cinderella."

At the end of their last working day, on the eve of the festival, Ella sat back in her chair, admiring her puppets. She was tired but still had the tingle of excitement she always felt the night before a holiday.

Val packed her own finished puppets into her wagon. For the first time, the girls hugged good-bye instead of shaking hands.

Val tucked Claudio into the flour satchel

and called out as she walked down the path, "Tomorrow is the big day! The village won't know what's coming to them. Cinderella and Valentine, master puppeteers!"

As Ella watched Val leave, her heart felt heavy. She was full of love for her new friend and for Claudio. Ella yearned to see Val's dreams come true as much as her own. But she was also confused. She didn't feel any different about her own goal. She still wanted that win and the dress that came with it.

Ella wondered, how could both of their dreams come true when they were competing against each other for one prize?

Chapter 8
An Appeal for Magic

Later that evening, after supper, Ella left a sleeping Bruno by the fireplace and made her way to the garden bench. She hadn't visited her corner of the garden since Val's visits had begun.

Ella's thoughts swirled around in her mind. Her dreams had always felt so clear and so much her own. But now they were mixed up with someone else's.

Ella sat down on the bench and faced the willow. This time she didn't stare and wait for the fairies to appear. She spoke to them. "Fairy Godmother, I know you're in there. My mother told me about you. That you're looking out for me. But I've found someone else who needs looking after. Her name is Val, and she has a pig named Claudio. I'm sure you'd like them. I didn't like her so much at first, but . . . never mind."

Ella thought about what she was asking for. "I thought since you have magic on your side, maybe you could help us. We both want to win the puppet contest tomorrow. I don't know how it's possible for both of us to get what we want. And even if Val wins, I fear it's not enough to reach her dream of a farm in the country. Can you help her get that farm, Fairy Godmother? At the very least, could you make sure we stay friends no matter who wins? Or help Sir Edgard to stop being so cruel?"

Ella had closed her eyes. She opened one, just a little, hoping she might see a fairy in a blue frock before her. Nothing. She opened both eyes. Still nothing.

Ella's shoulders fell. She didn't understand. Had her mother made it all up?

She felt a hand touch her shoulder. Without looking, she knew who it was.

"Ella, darling. She is there. She's always there."

"It doesn't look at all like she's there, Mother," Ella said.

Her mother sat down and took her hands. "Your fairy godmother will always be here for you. I promise you that much. You must

have faith. She will appear to you when you need her the most."

"When will that be?" Ella asked.

Her mother tucked a lock of hair behind Ella's ear. "I hope not anytime soon. But it's very kind of you to ask for help for Val."

"I didn't think it could hurt to try," Ella said.

"Of course not," Ella's mother said. "Though it may make you happy to know that Val's dreams have a magic and power of their own, as all dreams do. Why, I wouldn't be surprised if she has her own fairy godmother."

"Oh, that would be wonderful," Ella said.

"You don't always have to look to the willow tree." Ella's mother put her hand over Ella's heart. "Friendship and love have their own magical way of helping wishes come true."

Ella hoped her mother was right. A farm was such a big dream for someone who had to hide a tiny pig. And it seemed that one way or another, Val or Ella would end up disappointed by the end of the festival. But then Ella caught sight of the glowing castle towers in the distance and felt her heart leap. *Anything is possible,* she reminded herself.

And the possibilities would start tomorrow, when Mademoiselle Cinderella and Mademoiselle Valentine premiered their puppet shows at the Midsummer Festival.

Chapter 9
A Festival of Surprises

The next morning, Ella woke before the sun rose. The day of the festival had arrived. She felt as though one of her beloved bonfires were sparking up inside her chest. She rushed through her morning routine so she could begin loading her puppets into her father's wagon. Ella felt so impatient that she thought about trying to drive the horses herself while her father searched for his hat. But she didn't want to risk crashing the wagon and harming the puppets.

After what felt like forever, Ella, her mother, her father, Bruno, and the puppets headed toward the village. Ella's excitement swelled as they drew closer. She could hear the music, smell the treats, and see the colorful festival banners draped across the rooftops. As soon as her father pulled the wagon to a stop, Ella jumped down and ran to find the puppet booths.

She found Val with her mother, already setting up. "Cinderella, here!" Val pointed at the booth next to hers. "I made sure it stayed empty. Oh, and this is my mother."

Val's mother waved at Ella. She had the same dark hair as Val, and the same kind eyes and playful smile.

Ella returned her wave. "It's a pleasure to meet you, Madame. I've heard so much about you."

"As have I, love," Val's mother said. "I'm looking forward to seeing the shows you girls have cooked up in that barn. Val won't tell me a thing!"

Val's mother helped Val lift one of her puppets behind the booth. Ella noticed that it had a stick fastened to the bottom. Ella had wondered how Val was planning to operate it. Ella's puppets had places to hide a hand inside or strings attached. Val must have attached the stick when she left the barn, no doubt part of her much-talked-about "secret."

Ella's mother and father approached, her father carrying her crate of puppets. Ella got busy setting up in the booth next to Val's as her parents introduced themselves to Val's mother.

"Okay, everyone. Time to enjoy the festival and leave Mademoiselle Valentine and Mademoiselle Cinderella to their debuts. So long!" Val signaled for their parents to leave.

Ella's mother laughed and kissed Ella on the forehead. "Shine like the fairies are watching, my darling," she said.

"I'm proud of you, Ella," her father said. "Excuse me, I mean Mademoiselle Cinderella." He winked.

Val's mother whispered something into her daughter's ear that made Val light up in a way Ella hadn't seen before. Then the three grown-ups walked off into the crowd to explore the festival.

"Let's put on a show!" Val called to Ella. Within minutes, the girls had small crowds of children gathered in front of their booths. And put on a show they did.

Ella used her puppets to tell a story of a maiden who had fallen into a deep, dreamy sleep. When she awoke, she was lost in a strange forest. She searched and searched for a way out but only became more lost. She called out for help, and the only one who answered her was a well-dressed frog. When the maiden asked for directions, the frog danced a jig.

When the maiden asked his name, the frog spun in circles. When the maiden began to cry, the frog hopped and skipped. Through the maiden's tears, the frog continued to dance. The maiden became so tired of being sad that she decided to join him. The maiden and the frog danced and danced until the maiden began to laugh. A fairy appeared. She told the maiden that a terrible witch had cursed the frog, forcing him to do nothing but dance alone for years until he found a partner. The maiden had broken the spell with her dance. The fairy said that since the spell was broken, she would give the maiden three choices. She could turn the frog into a gentleman to keep the maiden company in the forest. She could turn the frog into a large bird to fly the maiden home. Or she could banish the frog and put a spell on the maiden to allow her to sleep and live in her dreams forever.

The maiden looked at the frog, who had helped her find laughter in a time of sorrow. She told the fairy she would not make a choice. She would rather keep the frog just the way he was. In the blink of an eye, the maiden found herself back home, the frog by her side. And they lived out the rest of their days as the very best of friends.

The children loved it. They had laughed, clapped, oohed, and aahed at all the right parts. As soon as that show ended, a new crowd formed to watch the next one.

Val's show seemed to be going just as well. Ella was too busy with her own show to watch, but she could hear children squealing with delight at Val's wacky-looking puppets. Everything was going just as the girls had hoped.

Throughout the day, Ella noticed a man walking back and forth between the puppet booths. Because of the chill she felt as he paused in front of her show, she was sure it was Sir Edgard. He was tall, with a pair of spectacles that seemed much too small on top of his protruding nose. He wore fine clothes, although they seemed dark and heavy for such a bright summer day.

Ella tried to ignore the anger she felt when she saw him, thinking of poor Claudio hiding back in the shack. As she continued dancing her puppets across the stage, it struck her: maybe Sir Edgard had something good in him, too. As her father had said, there was something good in everyone—and he had been more than right about Val.

Though the day was long, as all summer days are, before Ella knew it, the sun began to set. The festival torches lining the village were lit, including one behind Val's booth. Ella stepped away from her last show just in time to see the lighting of the grand bonfire in the center of the village square. The gathered crowd roared with applause. Ella felt her face brighten in the glow of the flames. The judging ceremony would begin at any moment, as it always did at sundown.

Ella glanced at Val to see if she'd noticed the fire. Ella was ready to call her over, but Val was rummaging around in her cart, looking for something.

Ella started toward Val's booth to offer a hand when Val shot up, holding a large piece of cloth. It was one of the curtains that used to hang in her shack to hide her puppets.

"Everyone!" Val clapped her hands loudly three times, drawing the attention of the

bonfire crowd. "Mademoiselle Valentine has one last show!" Val draped the curtain across the front of her puppet booth and disappeared behind it with a torch.

What could she possibly be doing? Ella wondered. This must be the trick Val had promised.

A shadow moved behind the curtain. It was dark and strong against the white cloth. Ella recognized the shape. It was one of Val's puppets, a long-limbed creature that looked like a cross between a spider and a hare. The shadowed limbs began to move, and Val's voice boomed into the crowd. She told a story about how the creature came to life.

Several more puppets appeared behind the curtain, all in shapes Ella recognized. None of the beautiful details—the metalwork or the clever use of flowers and trinkets—could be seen. In their place was something new: another level of puppetry and creation. Val had not only made puppets; she had made shadow puppets, using the Midsummer Festival torches as her stage lights. The audience was in awe of the shadow show, and Ella was, too.

When Val's performance was over, the crowd erupted in applause, whistles, and cheers. Val came out and took a bow, sneaking a grin at Ella. Ella grinned back. Val was right. She had had a trick, and there was no doubt in Ella's mind that she had won the contest. But before she could walk over to congratulate her, the trumpets sounded. The judging was about to begin.

All the puppeteers stood in front of their booths, their puppets lying limply on the small stages. Sir Edgard paced in front of them, back and forth, back and forth. He cradled the gold coin on his palm, its brilliance shining in the crackling light of the bonfire. When he reached Val's booth the third time, Ella puffed up her chest, ready to explode with cheers.

But Sir Edgard kept walking. He stopped between Val's and Ella's booths. He took a great dramatic pause as he faced the crowd, holding the gold coin up for everyone to see. "Ladies and gentlemen, your winner!" he announced.

And he grabbed Ella's hand and raised it in victory.

Chapter 10
An Important Voice

Ella couldn't believe her ears or the fact that her arm was raised in the air. She let her hand fall out of Sir Edgard's, only to see it holding the gold coin he had pressed into her palm. It was strange. Ella was holding the coin she'd been dreaming of in the garden for so long. But now it felt like a heavy stone in her hand.

"Congratulations," Sir Edgard said.

Ella was so stunned, she hadn't noticed that the crowd was clapping—clapping very politely. Ella was sure they knew, as she knew, that the wrong person had won. This didn't feel like victory to Ella. This should have been Val's victory.

Ella glanced over at her friend, expecting to see her upset. But she wasn't. Val was clapping louder and harder than anyone else, her face full of pride and true joy.

Ella looked up at Sir Edgard, who was nodding at the crowd. His face was pinched in an awkward smile. "But, sir," Ella began. "Surely, sir . . . did you miss Val, I mean,

Mademoiselle Valentine's show? How is it possible that she's not the winner?"

Sir Edgard cleared his throat. "I saw that child's puppets. They're not what this fine tradition is about. Fancy tricks like that light show can't disguise what those puppets are made of. . . . Garbage, scraps, nothing more." He spoke his words with such confidence and authority, Ella could have almost believed him. Almost, if she didn't know Val.

But she did know Val.

And Ella knew what to do. She felt her spirit return as she looked at her friend. She took a step toward Val, thinking about what she would name the goat, the first animal for her family's farm. But before Ella got very far, she was stopped in her tracks. A voice called out over the noise of the crowd. An important voice.

The voice of the king.

Chapter 11
A Message from the King

Not even in her daydreams had Ella pictured this: approaching her was the king. She fell into a deep curtsy.

"A marvelous show, child. Please, please, stand," the king said.

Ella did as he asked. "Thank you, Your Majesty," she said. She tried to look at him but was too nervous to meet his eyes. She looked at the top of his crown instead.

She'd never seen such gleaming gold or sparkling jewels. This would fuel her daydreams for a very long time.

"Congratulations on all your hard work." The king nodded at Ella and walked away.

Ella's breath caught in her throat. Could that really have happened? Words exchanged with the king? She saw her parents standing back in the crowd. Their eyes met, and Ella smiled.

"And you, young lady," the king said. The king was still talking! Ella turned sharply to see who he was addressing, and everyone in the crowd did, too.

Val. He was walking over to Val! Ella saw

her friend's face turn pink as she realized the king was speaking to her. She curtsied, too, so deeply that it looked like her knees might touch the cobblestones.

"Thank you, child." The king held out a hand and helped Val stand. "You had a magnificent show as well. Like nothing I've ever seen before."

Ella thought Val's eyes were going to pop out of her head. Val was speechless for the first time since Ella had met her.

The king turned to face the crowd. "It has given me great joy to see you all here at the Midsummer Festival today. This is one of my favorite celebrations of the year.

It fills my heart with pride to see what these children can do when they set their minds to it. Did everyone get a chance to see the puppet shows?"

The crowd whooped and applauded in response.

The king smiled. "I think what we've seen today, and especially this evening, demonstrates why our kingdom is one of the proudest and strongest in all the land. For years we've relied upon the talents of the cleverest and the brightest of our people. They don't spend our wealth on outside extravagance, but instead they build upon the rich resources we have here." The king put a hand on Val's shoulder. "This girl is a fine example of one of those people, the kind who have made this village and this kingdom as prosperous as it is today."

Ella wanted to run over to Val, grab her hand, and jump in delight at the king's praise. But she couldn't, as the king had Val's full attention. Ella watched Sir Edgard instead. His face turned a shade of dark crimson.

"Young lady." The king knelt down before Val.

"Mademoiselle Valentine," Val said.

The king let out an uproarious laugh.

Val smiled.

"Mademoiselle Valentine. I would be very grateful, and proud, if you would let me keep your puppets in the castle. I think they'd be wonderful entertainment for visitors from other kingdoms. Not to mention, I'd like to show them what a lucky king I am to have such brilliant subjects." The king reached into his robe. "This would be for a small fee, of course."

Val put her hand to her mouth and then quickly uncovered it. "Oh, yes, Your Majesty! I'd be honored!"

The king dropped a velvet pouch into Val's hands. Ella could hear the clinking of coins as it fell. Coins just like the one still warm in Ella's hand, but many, many more.

"Enjoy the bonfires, everyone!" The king waved at his subjects. Then, with his guards at his side, he disappeared into the crowd.

Ella ran over to Val and wrapped her in her arms. There was no doubt in her mind. Dreams were real, and they were coming true right now.

Chapter 12
A Rainbow of Dreams

Ella lounged on the garden bench, staring into the treetops and singing softly. She wasn't singing so the fairies would listen. She was singing so her heart would have a voice. She felt so full of happiness, full of wonder, and full of dreams come true. But stitched through these feelings was also a thread of sadness. In a few minutes she would be walking to the village to say good-bye to her friend.

As it turned out, the gold the king had given Val, together with Val's mother's savings, was enough for them to buy a small farm out in the country. Ella was amazed at how right her own mother had been. Val's dreams had made magic happen and had shown Ella that what she felt in the garden was true: Anything was possible.

"Would you like me to come with you, darling?" Ella heard her mother's voice behind her and smiled as she turned her head from the sky.

"I'll be all right, Mother. Bruno will be with me," Ella said as she stood.

"It's never easy to say good-bye to a friend. Especially one as wonderful and new as Val," Ella's mother said.

"No. I don't expect it will be. But I feel that it's not good-bye. Even if she's leaving . . . I know she's not really leaving me." Ella looked into her mother's eyes. "Does that sound like nonsense?"

Ella's mother shook her head. "Not even a bit."

"Come, Bruno!" At Ella's call, Bruno tore himself away from playing with the chickens and raced over.

Ella had just started for the village path

when she felt something placed in her hand. It was her mother's fan. "It's warm out here, Ella," her mother said. "Look after yourself."

Ella gripped the fan, opening it once and folding it up again. She'd always adored this fan. Its elegant beauty was so much like her mother's. "Thank you, Mother. I will," Ella said, kissing her on the cheek.

Ella and Bruno made their way toward the edge of the village, where the road into the western country began. Val and her mother were there, sorting and arranging their few belongings in a covered wagon they'd hired for their journey. The wagon was larger than Ella had expected. She

peeked inside to find cages of chickens, three pigs, two sheep, and a goose. And to her surprise, behind the wagon were two cows, chewing on the grass that lined the path.

"Val! There are so many animals. I thought the gold was only enough to start with the house!" Ella exclaimed.

Val hopped down from the front of the wagon. "You'll never believe it. When my mother told Sir Edgard our plan, he said there was no point for him to keep the animals without someone to look after them. So he sold them to us. All except his two prized pigs." Val lowered her voice to a whisper. "I think we may have cheated him. He took only three coins."

Ella frowned. "Sir Edgard hardly seems like the kind of man to let himself be taken advantage of. Perhaps he was being kind?"

Val thought for a moment. She lifted Claudio out of the wagon so he could say hello to Bruno, who'd been whining at her feet for the pig. "You know, when he made the deal, he did say I could keep the runt for free. So it seems he knew about Claudio all along."

"It's like my father said, Val. There's good in everyone. Even old Sir Edgard," Ella declared.

Val laughed. "Let's not get carried away."

"Everything's all set, girls. I need to run to the market for one last thing." Val's mother reached her arms out to Ella for a hug. "It's been a pleasure knowing you, Ella. Please come visit us anytime." She gave Ella a squeeze and left.

Val and Ella stood in silence. They watched Bruno and Claudio wrestle on the ground.

Val finally spoke. "It's true, you know. You can visit us anytime. I know it's not the same as walking down the path into the village, but it's only half a day's journey."

Ella nodded. "I noticed you don't have a goat in that wagon," she said.

"Oh, right. Well, we never had a goat on Sir Edgard's property. That's why I wanted one," Val said.

Ella pulled the gold coin out of her pocket. "I was hoping you might use this for a goat. For me, of course. It could be my goat. You could just look after it. And then I'd have another friend to visit."

Val beamed as she took the coin. "No dress after all?"

Ella shook her head. "A goat seems much more exciting."

Val clapped her hands. "If it's a goat you

want, then a goat you shall have!" And with that, she pulled Ella in close for a hug. They embraced for a while, and Ella felt a tear roll down her cheek. When they pulled apart, Ella could see that Val's eyes were wet, too.

"Don't be sad, Val. I'm so happy for you," Ella said, wiping away her tear.

"You've been a great friend, Ella," Val said, sniffling.

"So have you. And call me Cinderella. Anything else from you sounds funny." Ella giggled. "I'll miss you."

"I'll miss you, too," Val said. "But there's something my father used to say when I was little, before I knew I was going to miss him always. We can see each other in our dreams. Just wish for it in your heart, right before you go to sleep."

"It's a deal," Ella said.

"Deal," Val said. She called to Claudio and climbed into the wagon. "Oh! One more thing." Val pulled a package from the wagon and handed it to Ella. It was wrapped in paper. "Don't open it here."

Ella hugged the package to her chest. "Good-bye, Mademoiselle Valentine."

"Good-bye, Mademoiselle Cinderella." Val waved. With one last look, Ella trudged back to the chateau, Bruno at her heels.

When she returned home, she went straight to the garden. It felt like the only place she wanted to be just then. She'd hoped to save the present for later, but she missed Val so much already, she couldn't help herself.

Ella tore open the paper to find a puppet. It was made from a combination of Val's odds and ends and the scraps she had taken from Ella the first day they had met. Ella didn't know when Val had sneaked them away again, but it didn't matter. The puppet was a rainbow, cobbled together from all colors of metal, beads, wood, and lace. It was the most beautiful and hopeful thing Ella had ever seen or dreamed.